# LEGO® Friends

# The Heartlake Adventure

PUFFIN

PUFFIN BOOKS

Published by the Penguin Group
Penguin Books Ltd, 80 Strand, London WC2R 0RL, England
Penguin Group (USA) Inc., 375 Hudson Street, New York, New York 10014, USA
Penguin Group (Canada), 90 Eglinton Avenue East, Suite 700, Toronto, Ontario, Canada M4P 2Y3
(a division of Pearson Penguin Canada Inc.)
Penguin Ireland, 25 St Stephen's Green, Dublin 2, Ireland (a division of Penguin Books Ltd)
Penguin Group (Australia), 707 Collins Street, Melbourne, Victoria 3008, Australia
(a division of Pearson Australia Group Pty Ltd)
Penguin Books India Pvt Ltd, 11 Community Centre, Panchsheel Park, New Delhi – 110 017, India
Penguin Group (NZ), 67 Apollo Drive, Rosedale, Auckland 0632, New Zealand
(a division of Pearson New Zealand Ltd)
Penguin Books (South Africa) (Pty) Ltd, Block D, Rosebank Office Park, 181 Jan Smuts Avenue, Parktown
North, Gauteng 2193, South Africa

Penguin Books Ltd, Registered Offices: 80 Strand, London WC2R 0RL, England

puffinbooks.com

First published 2013
001

Written by Poppy Bloom
Illustrations by AMEET Studio Sp. z o.o.
Text and illustrations copyright © AMEET Sp. z o.o., 2013

Produced by AMEET Sp. z o.o. under license from the LEGO Group.

 AMEET Sp. z o.o.
Nowe Sady 6, 94-102 Łódź – Poland
ameet@ameet.pl  www.ameet.pl

LEGO, the LEGO logo and the Brick and Knob configurations
are trademarks of the LEGO Group.
©2013 The LEGO Group.

Set in Bembo.
Printed in Poland by AMEET Sp. z o.o.

British Library Cataloguing in Publication Data
A CIP catalogue record for this book is available from the British Library

ISBN: 978-0-72327-979-2

| | |
|---|---|
| Item name: | LEGO® Friends. The Heartlake Adventure |
| Series: | LBW |
| Item number: | LBW-102 |
| Batch: | 01 |

# The Heartlake Adventure

## Poppy Bloom

**Andrea**
Star Performer

**Mia**
Animal Lover

**Olivia**
Brilliant
Inventor

**Stephanie**
Social Butterfly

**Emma**
Stylish Designer

**Chelsea**
Uptown Girl

**Jacob**
Class Joker

# Contents

# 1
# A Cool Idea

Olivia wrapped her arms around herself and hurried down the street with her four best friends Emma, Stephanie, Andrea and Mia. School had just finished, and they were heading to their favourite hangout, the downtown bakery. "It's so cold I can't feel my toes anymore," Olivia said, laughing.

"I can't feel my whole body anymore!" Emma exclaimed.

Olivia could just make out Emma's sparkling eyes underneath her layers of wintry clothing. She had a stylish lavender beret pulled low

over her long, glossy black hair, and a scarf
wrapped all the way over her nose.

"I don't know what you guys are
complaining about. I love winter!" Stephanie
said, twirling the end of her scarf around her
hand. It was loosely looped around her neck
and her sporty parka wasn't even zipped all
the way up. Her long, blond hair fluttered in
the brisk wind blowing off the harbour and
through the streets of Heartlake City.

Andrea shivered. Only her big green eyes
and a wisp of curly dark brown hair were
visible between her knit hat and her long,
fuzzy gold-and-cream scarf. "You're crazy,"
she told Stephanie, her words muffled by
the scarf's thick wool. "What is there to love
about winter?"

"The crisp, clean air for one thing."
Stephanie breathed in deeply and smiled. "Plus

there's so much fun stuff to do! Like skiing, ice-skating, sledging, snowboarding ..."

"Freezing your nose off waiting for the bus," Mia added, pushing a strand of long

red hair out of her eyes. Then she started ticking off more items on her gloved fingers. "Stepping in puddles of slushy snow, shovelling the driveway…"

"Warm evenings by a crackling fire," Stephanie countered with a smile. "Piping hot chocolate…"

"Speaking of which, I hope there's plenty of that at the bakery," Emma added.

"I just hope the heat is turned up," Andrea said, huddling into her jacket.

Olivia nodded without answering. She was afraid her lips might be too frozen to say anything. Luckily, though, the bakery was just ahead. She hurried towards it, being careful not to slip on any stray patches of ice on the pavement.

The girls burst into the bakery's cosy
interior, with its cheerful aqua blue tables
looking warm and inviting. The big plate-
glass windows were fogged up from the heat
inside. The entire place smelled like freshly
baked cupcakes and coffee. The bakery's owner,
Danielle, was busy serving hot chocolate to
one of the customers.

"I'll go and order," Mia offered, unwrapping
her scarf. She got on well with the owner, so she
always made sure her friends got quick service.

"Thanks," Stephanie said. "Don't forget to
order us some muffins. All that nice, brisk
winter air has made me hungry."

As Mia hurried off towards the kitchen,
Olivia and her other friends headed over
to the only empty table, peeling off layers
as they went. As she shrugged off her jacket

11

and slid into the chair, Olivia heard someone
calling her name. She glanced up and saw
a girl sauntering towards the table. She had
wavy blonde hair and was dressed in a trendy
emerald-green hoody and designer jeans.

"Oh, hi, Chelsea," Olivia said, trying to
sound polite.

Chelsea Noble was one of the girls'
classmates from Heartlake High School.
Olivia always tried to be nice to her, but
sometimes it wasn't easy. Chelsea loved to
brag about everything, from her parents'
expensive cars to her high grades at school.
She was also a terrible gossip.

"What are you doing here, Olivia?" Chelsea
asked, tapping on the table with her perfectly
manicured fingernails. "I thought you'd be at
home figuring out what to do for your project."

"What's she talking about?" Andrea asked.
"What project?"

"Our extra-credit project for science
class," Olivia told her. "Ms Russell
said we could do something for our
technology unit, remember?"

Emma looked confused. "Sure, I remember.
But why are you doing an extra-credit project
in science, Olivia? You always get straight-A-
plusses in that class."

"I know." Olivia smiled. She loved science
class! "But the project sounds like fun. Besides,
I might need the extra credit to get into the
advanced science class next year."

"Yeah," Chelsea said loudly. She hated being ignored. "Olivia stayed after class to talk to Ms Russell about the project and so did I. She wants us to turn our projects in next Monday – one week from today."

"That doesn't give you much time," Stephanie said, pulling off her gloves. "So what are you going to do, Olivia?"

"I'm not sure yet," Olivia said. "I want to think of something really unique."

"Hmm." Chelsea didn't look impressed. "Well, I'm probably going to do a photo essay of all the cool technology we have at my house, like our new home theatre and my dad's fancy computer and stuff. I'm sure Ms Russell will be totally impressed."

Just then Mia arrived. She was carrying a tray with five steaming mugs of hot chocolate on it. A tray of muffins was balanced on her other hand.

"I asked Danielle to make everything extra hot," she said. "Since it's extra cold outside."

"It's not that cold," Chelsea said with a sniff. "At least not if you have a super warm coat like me."

"And super expensive," Emma muttered.

Chelsea shrugged. "You have to pay for quality, you know."

As she wandered off, Stephanie rolled her eyes. "Chelsea's photo essay sounds like just another way

to show off how rich she is," she said.
"I'm sure your project will be much more
interesting, Olivia."

Andrea nodded. "Do you have any ideas yet?"

"Ideas for what?" Mia asked as she
sat down. "What are you guys
talking about?"

Olivia filled her in. "I think I want to do
something that focuses on Heartlake City," she
said. "I mean, I haven't lived here as long as all
you guys have, but I already know there's lots
of technology here."

Stephanie grinned. "Why don't you do
a photo essay at Chelsea's house?"

The girls all laughed.

"No, thanks." Olivia blew on her drink to
cool it. "I was thinking I might do some sort
of computer program. Maybe a guide to all

the interesting new technology in Heartlake City, or something? I could include information about the best Wi-Fi spots in town, and the high-tech transport system…"

Mia looked worried. "Isn't there already something like that on the city's website?"

Stephanie nodded. "I helped the mayor launch it last year," she said. "It's pretty cool. It lists everything there is to do around here and lots of information about the city." She shrugged. "Including the technology stuff. Sorry, Olivia."

"Oh, well." Olivia slumped in her seat and sipped her hot chocolate. "I guess I'll have to think of something else."

"Too bad," Andrea said. "You're such a great computer programmer, I bet you could have done a brilliant job with something like that."

Emma was staring into space. Olivia wasn't sure she was even paying attention to the conversation until she spoke up. "You could still do a computer program," Emma said. "It would just have to be a little more creative."

Stephanie smiled. "Maybe you could help her with that. You're the most creative person I know."

Olivia nodded. It was true – Emma loved art, fashion design and interior decorating. And she was good at all of them. "Do you have any ideas for me, Emma?" Olivia asked.

Emma stirred her drink. "What if you make it a game?" she suggested. "Like those computer games where you build your own city and you add buildings and people. Only in this case, you could build Heartlake City!"

"But Heartlake City is already perfect," Andrea said, grabbing another muffin. "Why would anyone want to rebuild it?"

"That's true." Olivia thought about Emma's idea. "But maybe instead of rebuilding it, I could use the city as the setting for some other kind of game. That could be cool, right?"

"Definitely!" Stephanie sat up straighter. "Maybe the game could be fighting off aliens that are attacking Heartlake City!"

"Aliens?" Andrea wrinkled her nose. "I wouldn't want to play that kind of game. Maybe it could be some kind of talent show."

Olivia smiled. Andrea was a talented singer, actor and dancer — it wasn't surprising that she'd like to play a performing game. "Sounds fun, but it might be tricky to make a talent show work as a computer program," Olivia said. "Computerized characters aren't that good at singing and dancing."

"Anyway, it should be something that shows all of Heartlake City, not just the theatre," Mia said.

"Right," Stephanie said. "Like showing the aliens trying to destroy the entire place!"

"No aliens," Andrea said firmly. "It could be something else. Like, um…"

"A quest!" Olivia blurted out as the idea popped into her head. "That's my favourite type of game, anyway. You know — the kind where you have to solve puzzles and figure out clues that eventually lead you to a treasure or something."

Emma nodded thoughtfully. "That does sound cool."

"And the quest could lead you all through Heartlake City." Stephanie grinned. "It's perfect!"

"Definitely," Andrea agreed. "I can't wait to play it when it's finished!"

Mia nodded. "You have to promise to let us be the first ones to test it, OK?"

"Absolutely!" Olivia clapped her hands. "Now I'm even more excited about the project. I can't wait to go home and get started!"

"Are you sure about that?" Andrea glanced at the window. "It looks like it just started to snow."

Emma groaned. "Again? My feet are getting blisters from wearing my snow boots every day."

"Oh, come on," Stephanie said. "Seriously, you guys just have the wrong attitude about winter. You need to embrace it!"

Andrea looked dubious. "I'd rather embrace a trip to a hot and sunny place."

"Forget it!" Stephanie's blue eyes were taking on a gleam that Olivia recognized. It meant she was cooking up some kind of plan. "I'm going to figure out a way to prove to you guys that winter is awesome."

"If you say so." Mia took another sip of her hot chocolate. "I suppose if anyone can do it, it's you, Steph."

Olivia nodded. Stephanie was great at making things happen. Olivia's father called her "a real go-getter." She never let anything stand in her way once she came up with a plan.

But Olivia wasn't really thinking much about Stephanie's plans. She was focused on her own. Once again, her friends had helped her come up with a fantastic idea and Olivia knew she could turn it into the best extra-credit project ever.

She couldn't wait to get started!

# 2
# Olivia Gets Started

"May I please be excused?" Olivia wiped her mouth with her napkin and pushed away her empty dinner plate. "I want to go and start working on my project."

"Of course." Her mother looked up from her food. "It's your father's turn to clear the table."

Olivia's dad groaned. "Are you sure?"

Olivia smiled. "She's right, Dad. I took your turn when you had to stay late at the newspaper office because of that tight deadline, remember?"

"Oh, right." Her father smiled, his eyes twinkling. "Um, did I mention I have a tight deadline tonight, too?"

"Nice try, Peter," Olivia's mum said with a laugh. "Go ahead, Olivia. I'll help your dad clean up."

Olivia hurried up to her room. As usual, it was tidy but scattered with unusual things. Most of Olivia's gadgets, tools and interesting artifacts were in her invention workshop out in the garage, but a few always made it into the house. Today there was a screwdriver on the bedside table and an old bicycle chain on top of the bookshelf. Several pieces of a computer motherboard were scattered across the desk.

Olivia carefully moved the computer parts, then sat down and pulled out her laptop. She logged onto the Internet and searched for

a map of Heartlake City. It didn't take long
to find a good one, which she printed out on
her colour printer. After digging into her desk
drawer for some drawing pins, she pinned
the map to her bulletin board.

"This is going to be so cool," she whispered
as she stared up at the map.

Her eyes moved over the old town square
and the modern business district, the harbour
and beach, and the lush city park with the
sparkling waters of Lake Heart at the centre.
She would definitely have to include all of
those settings to make the virtual world of her
game feel like the real world of Heartlake City.

Pulling the computer closer, she got to work.
Her fingers flew over the keyboard, setting up
the basics of the game. Once that was finished,
she planned to move on to sketching out

the most important backgrounds using her favourite graphics program. After that, she could plan the details of the quest and start figuring out how to make the whole thing work.

She was focused on finding the right shade of blue for the water in the lake when her dog, Scarlett, pushed open the bedroom door and trotted in. Scarlett was carrying her lead in her mouth. Olivia stopped typing long enough to give the dog a pat.

"Hi, girl," she said. "Ready for your evening walk?"

Scarlett perked up at the word "walk." She dropped the leash at Olivia's feet and let out a little bark. Then she grabbed the leash again and wagged her tail.

"OK." Olivia had already started typing again. "Just give me a minute…"

Olivia was testing a command that made the trees in the game version of Heartlake Park sway in the breeze when she heard a strange buzzing noise. She leaned in to hear if it was coming from her computer. She frowned, hitting a few keys.

"That's weird," she murmured. "What's making that noise?"

BZZ! There it was again.

This time Olivia realized the sound wasn't coming from the computer after all. It was her mobile phone buzzing inside her backpack. She was so preoccupied with the game, she'd dumped the backpack on her bed after school and still hadn't taken anything out of it.

She hurried over and scrabbled through the backpack, finally answering the phone on the sixth ring. "Hello?"

"You're there!" It was Stephanie. "I was starting to think you weren't going to answer."

"Sorry." Olivia sat down on the edge of the bed. "I was working on my extra-credit project."

"Oh, right. How's it going?"

"Great so far." Olivia smiled as she thought back over everything she'd accomplished that evening. "I started by downloading a free game engine so I don't have to code everything

32

from scratch. Setting that up was easy and now I'm working on the graphics for the backgrounds. The programming is a little tricky, but I think I've figured it out. I have the park setting almost done. Next I want to create the business district and then after that I'll add more sections as I go along."

"Sounds good," Stephanie said. "Want to hear what I've been doing?"

"Sure." Olivia wandered over to her computer, staring at the trees she'd just created. Were they too tall? She would have to go to the park and check.

"OK." Stephanie sounded excited. "So remember how I promised to make you all love winter as much as I do? I had an idea about how to do it."

She paused. Olivia blinked, a little distracted. "What?" she said.

"I'm going to organize a whole week's worth of winter fun!" Stephanie announced, sounding excited. "I'm going to hand-pick a winter activity for each of you – something that you're sure to love. I figured I'd start with Mia. She's easy, right? If it has anything to do with animals, she'll adore it. So I was thinking I'd call the stable and set up a nice trail ride through the snowy woods. Doesn't that sound fun?"

"Um, sure." Olivia still wasn't paying that much attention to what Stephanie was saying. Her mention of Heartlake Stables had reminded her that she wanted to use it as one of the settings for her computer game. "But listen, can we talk about it tomorrow? I'm sort of in the middle of something…"

"Oh! Sorry," Stephanie said. "Sure, we'll talk at school tomorrow. See you then. And good luck with the project!"

"Thanks." Olivia clicked off the phone and tossed it on the bed, hurrying back to the computer.

A while later, Olivia's bedroom door opened again. This time her mother stuck her head in. "Time for bed, sweetheart," she said.

Olivia blinked and looked up from the computer screen. "Huh? But it's only…" She glanced at the clock on her computer. "Wow! Is it really nine already?"

"Uh huh." Her mother smiled. "And you have school tomorrow. So you'd better get some sleep."

Olivia stood up and stretched. Her shoulders felt stiff from bending over the computer for so long.

Suddenly she remembered something. "Oh, no!" she blurted out. "I was going to take Scarlett for a walk, but I guess she left."

"Your father took her out. We didn't want to

disturb you when you were working so hard
on your project."

"Oh. Thanks." Olivia still felt a little guilty.
She knew the lively dog loved her evening
walks. Olivia would have let Scarlett jump
in the snow drifts and chase the flakes falling
from the sky as much as she wanted, instead
of hurrying through the walk as her parents
often did.

Then she yawned and decided she was too
tired to worry about that.
She'd make it up to Scarlett by
taking her for an extra-long
walk tomorrow.

"Goodnight, Mum," she said.

"Goodnight, Olivia."
Her mother shut the door
behind her.

Olivia wandered towards the closet to get her pajamas. But she stopped halfway there to look out of the window. Thick grey clouds blocked the light of the moon, but the glow of the streetlight on the corner illuminated the fat snowflakes falling from the sky. The soft white layer of snow made everything look beautiful.

"Maybe Steph's right," she murmured
to herself. "There are a few good things
about winter."

Then her gaze wandered to the city skyline,
which was hazy and indistinct in the snowy
night. Olivia squinted at a glass and steel
building. Oops! She'd forgotten to include the
hospital where her mother worked!

"I definitely can't leave that out,"
she whispered.

Hurrying back over to her desk, she opened
the laptop again and started typing.

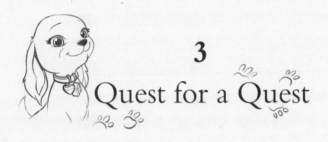

# 3
# Quest for a Quest

On Tuesday morning Olivia yawned all
through her morning classes. She'd stayed up
for another hour the night before. Finally her
dad had looked in and chased her off to bed –
right in the middle of finalizing the placement
of City Hall. Olivia had set her alarm to wake
her up half an hour early so she could finish
before breakfast. She hadn't had much sleep,
but it was worth it. Her backgrounds were
all laid out. All she had to do was fill in a few
more colours and details.

That meant it was time to figure out the quest that would tie the game together. She was thinking about it when she arrived in the cafeteria for lunch. Her friends were already at their usual table.

"I was sure school would be cancelled today after all the snow we got last night," Andrea was saying when Olivia sat down between Mia and Stephanie.

Emma unwrapped her cheese sandwich. "It's supposed to snow again this afternoon. Maybe we'll have the day off tomorrow."

"I hope so." Olivia opened her lunch bag and pulled out a carton of milk. "I could use the extra time. My project is pretty complicated and it needs to be finished by Monday."

"Oh, that's right!" Mia turned to her with a smile. "How's the game going so far?"

"Great! But there's still a lot to do." Olivia sipped her milk. "The programming takes a long time. The design work, too. I want everything to look perfect."

"I'm sure it will be great," Stephanie said. "You can do anything you set your mind to, Olivia!"

Olivia hardly heard her. "I have a few ideas for how my quest is going to work, but I need to figure out the details," she continued. "I might walk around the city this afternoon to get some inspiration."

"Can you do it tomorrow instead?" Stephanie sounded worried. "Because I already made plans for us this afternoon. Remember?"

"What kind of plans?" Andrea asked, glancing up from her lunch. "I hope it doesn't involve going outside and freezing our noses off."

Stephanie grinned. "Don't worry, you and your nose won't even notice the cold. We're going on a fabulous winter trail ride!"

"Really?" Mia sounded interested. "That could actually be fun. I haven't been on a horse since it started snowing last weekend."

"I know. I called the stables and they think it's a great idea," Stephanie said. "Getting out there and enjoying the beautiful winter scenery will be just the thing to show you guys that winter can be beautiful – and fun."

Andrea looked doubtful. "If you say so," she said. "Will I have time to go home and put on my warmest riding jodhpurs?"

"I have an extra pair of long johns if you want to borrow them," Emma offered. She glanced towards the cafeteria window, which was laced with frosty patterns. "Although maybe I should wear both pairs myself."

Stephanie grinned. "You guys can wear whatever you want. Just make sure you show up at the stables."

"Oh! Speaking of the stables, I had some trouble remembering all the details about it

when I was working on my project last night."
Olivia pulled out a notebook where she'd
been jotting notes on her project all day. "Mia,
do you know exactly how many stalls there
are in the main barn? And what colour is the
water trough outside the back door?"

For the next few minutes, Mia did her
best to answer Olivia's questions about
Heartlake Stables.

"Are those all your questions?"
Stephanie sounded a tiny bit
impatient. "Because we
should figure out what
time to meet this
afternoon."

"In a second, OK?"
Olivia was flipping
through her

45

notebook. "As long as we're all here, I have some questions for you about the flight school, too…"

By the time Olivia had answers to all of her queries, the bell was ringing to end lunch break. "Oops," Olivia said. "I guess we never got to talk about the trail ride. Sorry about that."

"It's all right." Stephanie smiled as she gathered up her things. "It's cool that you're so passionate about this project. We can make plans later."

Olivia headed straight home after school. Her head was buzzing with all the new ideas for her project. She couldn't wait to incorporate them into the game program.

As she unlocked the front door of her house,

she heard whining and panting from inside. The moment the door swung open, Scarlett leaped out at her, barking happily. Olivia always took the dog out for a long walk right after school, since both her parents worked all day. Normally it was fun, but today she wished there was someone else who could do it.

Unfortunately neither of her parents would be home until after five o'clock.

She grabbed Scarlett's leash off its hook near the door. "It's got to be a short walk today, OK, girl?" she said. "I have a lot to do."

Scarlett seemed disappointed when Olivia dragged her back inside after only ten minutes. The little dog followed as she hurried upstairs.

Olivia tossed her backpack on the bed and sat down at her desk. As she opened the laptop, she was smiling.

"I had a great idea for the quest, Scarlett," she told the dog.

Scarlett's tail thumped against the floor and she barked.

Olivia smiled. "Did you just say you want to hear my great idea? OK, I'll tell you. I'm going to have my players go all around Heartlake City searching for hidden objects. Once they find all the objects, they'll have to put them together like a puzzle to create something else." She winked at the dog. "I can't tell you what they create, though. I don't want you to give away the secret!"

Scarlett barked again, then jumped up against Olivia's legs. She nosed at the edge of the laptop.

"No, no," Olivia scolded. "Down, Scarlett. I need to concentrate now, OK?"

She opened her desk drawer and pulled out one of Scarlett's favourite dog toys. Tossing it into the hallway, she waited until the dog rushed over and pounced on it. Then she shut the door.

"It's OK, Scarlett!" she called as the dog whined and scratched at the door. "We can play in a little while."

Some time later, Olivia's phone rang. As she was reaching for it, she glanced at the time and gasped. She was supposed to meet her friends at the stables in less than five minutes!

"I'm so sorry, Steph!" she said as she answered the phone. "I totally lost track of the time, and –"

"Never mind that," Stephanie said. "Have you looked out of the window lately?"

"No, why?" Olivia wandered over to the window and pulled back the curtain. It was snowing hard – another two or three inches had fallen while Olivia was focused on her work.

"The trail ride's postponed." Stephanie sounded disappointed. "The owner of the stables is afraid it might be too icy on the trails right now."

"Oh. That's too bad." But secretly, Olivia's heart soared. She'd been worried about taking time away from her project to go on a trail ride. Now she could work on the game all night! "I'm sure we can ride some other time," she added.

"Definitely." Stephanie sounded determined. "And we're going to do lots of other fun winter stuff, too! I already have some ideas for something that will make Andrea feel a lot better about winter."

"That's great," Olivia said. "Um, but can we talk about it later? I'm kind of in the middle of an important bit of programming, and –"

"Sure." Stephanie cut her off. "That's fine. Bye."

She hung up. Olivia stared at the phone. Was it her imagination, or had Stephanie sounded a teensy bit annoyed just now?

Then she shook her head and clicked off the phone. Of course Stephanie was annoyed – but only because she'd had to postpone that trail ride. She'd be back to her usual cheerful self before long.

"OK, back to work," Olivia told herself, turning towards her desk.

# 4
# A Wintertime Walk

"It's not fair," Andrea grumbled the next day at lunch. "I was sure they'd cancel school this time!"

Stephanie laughed. "No way. They wanted us to get outside and see all the gorgeous new snow on our way here."

"Actually, it's probably because Heartlake City has such good public services," Olivia said. "I looked up some information on the city website last night and there was a whole page about the new snowplough the mayor approved last year."

Just then Chelsea hurried over to their table. "Hi, girls," she said. "Olivia, how's your project going? Mine's almost done."

"Really?" Olivia felt a pang of worry. She definitely had a lot more work to do on her extra-credit project. And it was already

Wednesday – that left her only four and a half days to finish. "Um, that's great, Chelsea. Mine's going fine."

"Yeah," Emma said. "Her game's going to be amazing!"

"Game?" Chelsea's sharp brown eyes darted from Emma to Olivia. "What do you mean, game? It's supposed to be a technology project."

Stephanie looked up from her salad. "Yeah, and a computer game is technology. Duh."

"Whatever." Chelsea rolled her eyes. "I seriously doubt some silly video game is what Ms Russell wants."

Chelsea's voice was always pretty loud, but it got even louder when she was annoyed. Four boys at the next table looked over curiously.

One of them, Jacob, jumped up and hurried over. "What are you guys talking about? What video game?" He was in the girls' science class and loved video games, too – no wonder he was so excited!

"Olivia's making a computer game based on Heartlake City," Mia explained. "It's going to be awesome."

"Really?" Jacob grinned. "Sounds cool. Am I in it?" Olivia stared at him. "Um, I don't know," she said. "I hadn't really thought about putting real people in the game."

"You totally should, though!" Andrea
sounded excited. "I mean, it wouldn't be
Heartlake City without all of us, right?"

"Including me," Jacob said.
"You can even make me
a superhero if you
want." He lifted
both arms and
flexed his
muscles in
a bodybuilder
pose.

Chelsea just
rolled her eyes.
"You can leave me out," she said. "You'd
never be able to get the exact shade of my
eyes right anyway." She stomped off towards
her own table.

Jacob helped himself to one of Emma's
cookies. "You can make my eyes any colour
you want as long as I have the power to fly."

"I'll think about it." Olivia smiled at him as he waved and headed back to his own table.

"If you put me in your game, make sure I'm a really awesome singer, OK?" Andrea struck a pose, pretending to hold a microphone.

Stephanie pointed at her with a carrot stick. "That reminds me," she said. "I need to talk to you guys about the next event in my plot to make you all love winter."

"Let me guess," Mia joked. "You're going to make us go outside and have a snowball fight."

"Actually, that sounds like fun." Stephanie grinned. "But no, I'm trying to do stuff you guys will like, not stuff I'd like."

"OK, so what are we doing?" Emma asked.

Stephanie's grin got bigger. "A fabulous concert of winter songs, featuring our very own superstar singer, Andrea!"

"Really?" Andrea sat up and patted her hair. "Actually, that does sound like fun."

"Yeah," Mia agreed.

"And it's indoors away from the snow and cold," Emma added. "That's my favourite part!" She shot a look at Andrea. "Um, I mean my second-favourite part. Your singing's always my favourite part."

"Cool, then it's settled." Stephanie looked pleased. "I asked Marie to let us do it at the café today at four. Can you all make it then?"

"Sure," Andrea said as Mia and Emma nodded.

"Olivia?" Stephanie turned. "What about you?"

Olivia hesitated. "Well, I was planning to walk around this afternoon and figure out cool places to hide my clues and puzzle pieces in the game."

Stephanie shrugged. "No problem, that won't take you too long, right?" she said. "But

60

we can push the concert back until four thirty if you want."

"Um, thanks." Olivia had been planning to ask if they minded if she skipped the concert. But her friends were being so nice that she didn't dare. "Four thirty should be fine."

"Great!" Stephanie pulled a sheet of paper out of her pocket. "OK, Andrea, I came up with a list of some good winter songs. Here – let me know which ones you want to do and I'll make sure they're cued up on the karaoke machine at the café."

"OK," Andrea said, taking the list and scanning it. "Wow, I never realized there were so many fabulous songs about winter."

Emma peered over her shoulder. "Ooh, look – 'Snow Party' by Piper Page. You have to do that one – it's my favourite!"

"A-ha!" Stephanie grinned. "I caught you – you both just admitted to liking something about winter!"

As all four of her friends laughed, Olivia gulped down the last of her lunch. "You guys have fun," she said. "I think I'll head over to the school library and use the computers there to do a little more research for my project."

Andrea waved the paper. "Don't you want to help us with the song list for the concert?"

"That's OK." Olivia slung her backpack over her shoulder. "It'll be more fun if it's a surprise."

Her friends exchanged a look. "OK, if you say so," Andrea said. "See you later."

Everything in Heartlake City sparkled in the
sunlight as Olivia wandered along Main Street.
The snow had been cleared off the roads and
pavements, but it still covered roofs, awnings
and other surfaces, and there were pretty icicles
hanging everywhere. Despite the cold, plenty
of people were hurrying in and out of the
boutiques and restaurants that lined both sides
of the street.

Olivia had left school as soon as the final
bell rang, wanting to spend as much time as
possible scouting locations for her game before
she had to meet her friends for the concert at
the café. She was determined to come up with
tricky and interesting spots to hide her clues in
the virtual version of the city she was creating.
She'd started by exploring the oldest part

of the city near City Hall and now she was checking out the more modern shopping and business districts.

She paused and stared at the colourful front window of a vintage store. It was one of Emma's favourite places to search for retro treasures she could recycle into current fashion trends. Thinking about Emma reminded Olivia of Jacob's question about using real people in the game.

"I should do it," she murmured with a smile. She'd been planning to let players create their own avatars to use in the game. But it might be even more fun if they got to play as real Heartlake City residents – like Olivia and all her friends!

"At least I won't have to do any research to create virtual versions of my friends," she thought as she moved on, squinting at the Heartlake Theatre on the next block. Seeing the theatre reminded her of Andrea, who had acted in a couple of productions there.

And thinking of Andrea reminded Olivia to check the time. Her watch was hidden under several layers of winter clothes, so she hurried forward until she could see the old clock tower atop City Hall.

She gasped when it came into view. It was almost four thirty. She was going to be late for the concert!

# 5
# New Ideas

Olivia burst into the café, out of breath from running the whole way there. Her friends were gathered near the small stage at one end of the room. Andrea was wearing one of her favourite performance outfits, a sparkly gold top and white mini-skirt. She and Emma were watching while Stephanie and Mia fiddled with the speakers.

"Oh good, you're here!" Stephanie exclaimed when she spotted Olivia. "We were afraid you forgot."

"No way." Olivia collapsed into a chair near the stage. "I said I'd be here, right? Sorry I'm a little late."

"It's OK," Andrea said. "We're running a little late, too."

"Yeah. Can you take a look at these speakers?" Mia straightened up and brushed

a strand of red hair out of her face. "They're all staticky."

"Sure." Olivia sneaked a peek at her watch as she bent over the speakers. If the concert ran too late, she might not have time to work on the game before dinner. And she really wanted to add in her latest ideas while they were fresh in her mind.

Pushing those thoughts aside, she focused on the speakers. It only took her a moment to discover that one of them had a loose wire.

"There," she said as she tightened it. "It should work fine now."

"Thanks, Olivia." Stephanie sounded relieved. "We can always count on you to fix things."

"No problem." Olivia gave a little salute. "Um, so what are we waiting for? On with the show!"

Stephanie grinned. Grabbing the microphone, she stepped up onto the small stage. "Welcome to a winter concert extravaganza, ladies and gentlemen!" she cried. "Please welcome the star of our show – the one and only, super-talented Andrea!"

Marie dimmed the lights and the other customers in the café applauded. Jacob whooped loudly and pumped his fist. He was sitting in a booth with several of his friends. "Go, Andrea!" he shouted as Andrea took the microphone from Stephanie.

"Thank you very much," Andrea said. "I'm going to start with an old favourite called 'Winter Fun'…"

After that, Andrea sang a whole list of songs about snow, cold and winter. The audience sang along with some and listened quietly to others. Everyone was having a good time, but Olivia found it hard to focus on the music. She kept thinking about her game.

Finally Andrea finished her last number. "Thank you, you've been a wonderful audience!" she called out, waving and smiling.

"Encore! Encore!" Jacob shouted, jumping to his feet.

"You're not going to do any encores, are you?" Olivia asked as Andrea came down from the stage and grabbed her water bottle.

"I don't know." Andrea's face was flushed with excitement and her eyes were sparkling. "I was thinking about it. Can you guys think of any more winter songs?"

"No," Olivia said quickly.

"Sure, I know lots more," Stephanie said. "But first, will you admit that you had fun tonight?"

"Of course." Andrea took a drink from her bottle. "That was a blast!"

Mia smiled. "You were right, Stephanie. Maybe there is at least one good thing about winter."

"Yeah," Emma agreed. "Sitting inside and listening to songs about it."

Stephanie laughed. "That's great. And I'm sure you guys will like the next activity just as much."

"Another activity?" Olivia gulped. She didn't have time for any more concerts or trail rides until her project was done. "But I thought you proved your point – that winter can be OK."

Stephanie ignored her. "Next, we're doing something to show Emma that there are some truly great things about winter," she announced. "Since I know you love anything artsy, Emma, we're entering the snow sculpture contest in the park tomorrow afternoon."

"The what?" Andrea asked. "You mean we're going to build a snowman?"

"No way!" Stephanie waved a hand. "We'll never win with a boring old snowman."

Emma looked interested. "I saw some pictures of the winners of that contest in the newspaper last year," she said. "It looked really cool."

"I saw it, too." Mia nodded. "Someone even built a half-scale replica of Heartlake Harbour lighthouse."

Olivia's eyes widened. She'd forgotten all about the picturesque old lighthouse across from Ambersands Beach. It would make a terrific location for one of the hidden objects in her game!

As the others talked excitedly about the snow sculpture contest, she cleared her throat. "Listen, I have to go," she said, her mind already coming up with ways to work the lighthouse into her plans. "I just had a new idea for my project and I want to add it before I forget."

"Oh." Andrea glanced at the stage. "You aren't going to stay for my encore?"

"Do you mind?" Olivia smiled at her hopefully.

Andrea shrugged and shot her a small smile. "I guess not. Good luck with your new idea."

"Yeah," Stephanie added. "I'll fill you in about the snow sculpture plans tomorrow."

"Thanks, guys. You're the best!" Olivia rushed out of the café without a backwards glance.

# 6
## Snow Day

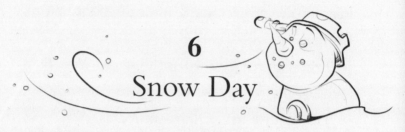

On Thursday morning Olivia woke up to the sound of sleet pattering against her windows. She got up and looked outside. The whole world seemed to be covered in ice!

When she went downstairs, her father was pouring himself a cup of coffee. He was still dressed in his bathrobe and slippers.

"Good news, Olivia," he said with a smile. "The mayor just announced that all schools in Heartlake City are closed today. And I've decided to work from home – the roads are too slippery to be safe."

"Great!" Olivia's eyes lit up. This gave
her a whole day to work on her project!
"Where's mum?"

"She had to go into work." Her father stirred
his coffee. "The hospital has to keep working
even if the rest of us get a snow day."

"You mean a sleet day." Olivia grinned and
grabbed a bagel out of the bread box. "I'll be
in my room."

"Going back to sleep?" her father asked.

"Nope. I've got work to do!"


Olivia's phone rang at eleven o'clock, startling
her out of designing the game's opening
screen. She grabbed the phone and answered
without checking to see who was calling.

"Hello?" she said, one hand still working the
mouse on her computer.

"Hi, Olivia. It's me," said Stephanie's familiar voice. "Bad news – they postponed the snow sculpture contest until next week."

"Really?" Olivia grinned. This really was her lucky day! "Um, that's too bad."

Stephanie didn't answer for a moment. "You could at least try to sound disappointed," she said at last.

"Sorry," Olivia said quickly. "It's just that I've got so much left to do on my game. I'll be able to have lots more fun with that contest next week."

"Oh, right." Stephanie sounded much less disgruntled. "I understand. Sorry, guess I'm just in a bad mood because I was all excited about the contest. So do you have time to take a break and meet us at the bakery later? I was just talking to Emma and we're both seriously craving some hot chocolate."

Olivia bit her lip, glancing at the computer screen. "I think I'd better not," she said. "I still have to finish the user interface stuff and I haven't even started designing the avatars yet and…"

"OK, OK," Stephanie said. "Never mind. We'll have some extra hot chocolate for you, OK?"

"Sounds good. Thanks," Olivia said, her mind already back on the game.

Olivia couldn't stop yawning as she walked into school on Friday morning. She'd been up until late working on her game.

She spotted her friends gathered in their usual spot near their lockers. When she joined them, they were talking about their day off.

"I spent the whole day reorganizing my closets," Emma was saying. "I sorted out my

winter clothes and gathered up a load of stuff
I never wear any more to donate to charity.

"Cool," Andrea said. "I slept late, then my
mum and I made cookies and popcorn and
watched some old movies."

"Awesome!" Stephanie smiled. "I wrote
an article for the newspaper in the morning,
then went cross-country skiing with my dad
in the afternoon."

"You mean you went out in that horrible
weather on purpose?" Mia leaned against her
locker. "I stayed inside and cleaned out my fish
tank and all my other pets' cages, then caught
up on reading all my animal magazines."

"Wait," Olivia said. "Didn't you guys go to
the bakery?"

"Nah." Emma shrugged. "Steph said you
didn't want to go. It didn't seem worth going

out in the yucky weather unless we were all going to be there."

"Oh." Olivia felt bad for a second. Then she remembered that she had good news. "Well, I won't have to skip any more activities from now on," she announced with a smile. "Because I finished my game!"

Emma gasped. "You did?"

"That's amazing!" Andrea exclaimed.

Mia patted Olivia on the back. "Congratulations."

"When do we get to play it?" Stephanie added.

"Today," Olivia said. "If you want to, that is. I thought we could all hang out at my house after school and you could beta test it for me. I really want to make sure there are no errors before I hand it in on Monday." She smiled

hopefully. "What do you say? Will you guys come?"

Stephanie grinned. "Just try to keep us away!"

"Yeah," Mia said. "You've spent so much time working on this game – it's sure to be amazing."

Andrea nodded. "I can't wait to try it!"

"Great." Olivia shivered with anticipation. "I can't wait, either. I think you guys are going to love it!"

# 7

# The Big Debut

"Come on in." Olivia swung open the door to her father's home office. "Dad said we can use his computer. It has a much bigger screen, so you'll be able to see the game a lot better."

"Cool." Stephanie rushed over and flopped into the desk chair. "I call first game!"

Olivia laughed. "Don't worry, you can all play at once," she said. "I set it up for as many as four players. You'll take turns moving around and looking for clues. Just let me get it set up…"

While Olivia plugged in the flash drive containing the game, Stephanie spun around in

the chair to face the others. "By the way,
I have a surprise for you guys," she announced.
"Since Olivia's finally finished with her
project, I set up another winter activity for us
this afternoon."

"Really? What is it?" Andrea asked.

Stephanie smiled. "It's a surprise. You'll see
when we get there."

"OK, it's ready," Olivia said. The intro
page flashed into view showing a big title
'Welcome to Heartlake City' on the computer
screen.

Emma gasped. "Oh, Olivia. It looks amazing!"

Olivia smiled. She had to agree – her game
really did look great. The opening screen
showed the Heartlake City skyline with the
sunset behind it. The name of the game –
THE HEARTLAKE ADVENTURE – was
spelled out in the sky in fancy letters.

Stephanie grabbed the mouse and clicked on the Start box. Another screen popped up. This one had a list of names.

Andrea smiled. "Hey, that's us!" she said, pointing to her own name. Emma, Mia and Stephanie were also listed.

"You made us characters in the game like Jacob suggested?" Mia asked, sounding pleased. "Cool."

Olivia nodded. "You can each play as yourselves if you want." She leaned forward and hit a few keys to set it up. Then she started the game. "Stephanie, you can go first."

"Awesome." Stephanie leaned forward eagerly as her avatar appeared on the screen.

Emma peered over her shoulder. "It looks just like you, Steph," she said. Then she squinted. "What are you holding?"

Olivia grinned. "It's a clipboard," she said. "Go ahead, move the mouse to make her walk."

Stephanie did as she said. On the screen, the game version of Stephanie raced forward at top speed. "Whoa!" the real Stephanie exclaimed. "Why's she going so fast?"

"I wanted to make her realistic," Olivia said. "And you're almost always in a hurry."

Mia laughed. "She's right about that. Ooh — look out, Steph!"

On the screen, Stephanie's avatar crashed into a streetlight. The figure stopped and reached for something hanging around her neck.

"What's she doing?" Emma wondered.

A second later, there was a shrill sound coming from the speakers. The avatar was blowing a whistle at the streetlight!

"Get out of the way!" the avatar ordered in a slightly tinny and very bossy computerized voice. "I'm busy!"

"That's the end of your turn," Olivia said. "When the time is up, the next person gets to go."

"That's me," Andrea said as another avatar popped up. She perched on the computer chair next to Stephanie. "Wait, what am I wearing?"

Emma leaned closer to look. "Is that a feather boa?"

Sure enough, Avatar Andrea was dressed in a slinky rhinestone-studded mini-dress with a hot-pink feather boa

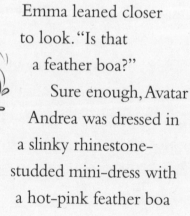

90

around her neck. A cordless microphone was clutched in one hand. Whenever Andrea moved the mouse, the avatar danced forward, bobbing her head, waving her arms, and adding in a dramatic twirl every time she stopped.

Mia laughed. "You're going to have trouble keeping up with Speedy Stephanie like that," she told Andrea.

"Don't be jealous of my cool moves," Andrea joked. She moved her avatar forward again. "How do I search for the treasures or whatever?" she asked Olivia.

"Just move through the city and look for anything that seems to be out of place," Olivia explained.

"OK." Andrea moved her avatar forward again, then frowned. "How do I make her stop dancing?"

Just then another person wandered into the scene. It was a lady pushing a baby stroller. As she came closer, Avatar Andrea turned towards her and burst into song. Olivia had sampled a few bars of one of Andrea's real concerts.

"Why's she doing that?" Stephanie asked in surprise.

Olivia shrugged. "I was just trying to make the avatars seem like you guys," she said. "Andrea loves to sing, right?"

Andrea moved her avatar away from the

lady and baby, which finally caused her to stop
singing. As she reached the corner, the avatar
stopped and flung a hand against her head.

"Wherever shall I go next?" the avatar said in
a dramatic voice.

"I don't sound like that," Andrea protested,
turning to glare at Olivia. As she did, she
moved her hand on the mouse. Her avatar
stepped forward with a dramatic shriek and the
turn was over.

"You next," Olivia told Mia.

Andrea got up to let Mia take her spot in
front of the computer. Mia's avatar appeared.
She was holding three leashes with a dog at the
end of each of them. A cat was perched on one
shoulder and a parrot on the other.

"What's that stuff falling off her?" Emma
asked, pointing.

"I think I know."
Mia leaned closer.
"It's pet hair."
Mia's turn didn't last any longer than the others'. Her avatar moved even more slowly than Andrea's, especially since the dogs stopped to lift their legs at every fire hydrant and lamp post. Her turn was up when Mia turned the avatar too suddenly, causing her to trip over one of the leashes.

"I guess I'm next," Emma said, taking her seat at the computer. "I can't wait to see what I'm wearing."

Her avatar appeared on the screen. She was
dressed in a puffy purple, green and gold dress.
The skirt stuck straight out on both sides. The
avatar's dark hair was piled high on top of
her head with all sorts of feathers and sparkly
things sticking out of it like a weird crown.

"What in the world is that?" Mia said.

Olivia shrugged. "I found a picture of that
outfit in a fashion magazine," she said. "It's
from a big runway show in Paris. Emma always
likes to dress in the latest styles, so…"

She let her voice trail off. None of her
friends said a word. They all watched as
Emma carefully moved her avatar forward.
The avatar tottered on her tall stiletto heels.
Her movements were a little wobbly and
Emma stopped her just in time to keep her
from walking into a wall.

As soon as she'd stopped, the avatar pulled a paintbrush out of the folds of her dress. She quickly painted a flower on the wall in front of her.

"Ooh, pretty!" Emma said.

The avatar put the brush away. She started turning in a circle. "Oh dear," she said in her computerized voice. "Where in the world was I going?"

"Why's she saying that?" Stephanie sounded confused.

"She's supposed to be an absent-minded artist," Olivia explained. "Sort of like you, Emma."

"Am I really that bad?" Emma's lower lip trembled.

"Of course not," Mia said quickly. "Olivia just exaggerated stuff about us for the game."

"A lot," Andrea added.

Stephanie checked her watch. "You know, we should probably get going," she announced. "I have that activity scheduled for us, remember?"

Olivia was surprised. "But we've barely started playing," she said. "I was hoping you guys could test more of it."

"Maybe later." Emma stood up. "I could use some fresh air."

Before she quite knew what was happening, Olivia was pulling on her coat and following her friends out into the cold winter afternoon.

# 8
# Stephanie's Suprise

As the five friends walked through the snowy streets of Heartlake City and boarded the bus, Stephanie kept up a steady stream of chatter. Olivia guessed that she was trying to distract the others so they wouldn't try to figure out where they were going. But she wished she'd be quiet for a moment. She wanted to ask her friends what they'd thought of the game. For some reason, they hadn't seemed quite as excited about it as she'd hoped. Nobody had even mentioned it since leaving her house.

Mia peered out of the window as the bus made a turn. "Hey, this is the road to the stables."

"Are we going on that winter trail ride after all?" Emma asked Stephanie. "I wish you'd told us. My riding boots are at home."

Stephanie grinned. "We're not going on a trail ride. You'll have to wait until we get there to find out what we're doing."

Olivia opened her mouth to ask about her game. Before she could get a word out, Mia started talking about an upcoming maths test. Olivia closed her mouth and sat back in her seat. She'd have to ask the others about the game later.

The bus dropped the girls off a short distance from Heartlake Stables. They walked the rest of the way, kicking bits of snow and ice off the pavement.

When they walked up the drive, Olivia's eyes widened. One of the stable workers was standing in front of the barn holding the bridle of a dark brown horse. Olivia recognized him right away. His name was Niki. He was one of the strongest and gentlest horses at Heartlake Stables.

Today Niki looked extra impressive all kitted out in full harness. Behind him was a large, gorgeous white sleigh. The runners curved up gracefully and were decorated with golden curlicues. Inside the sleigh, plush velvet cushions lined the benches and a cozy woollen blanket was slung over the side.

Emma clapped her hands. "A horse-drawn sleigh ride!" she exclaimed. "I love it! It's the perfect snowy day activity."

"Definitely." Mia smiled and gave Stephanie a hug. "You're the best! Thanks for organizing this, Steph."

Stephanie hugged her back. "You're welcome. Come on, let's climb aboard. You're driving!"

All five girls piled into the sleigh. Olivia ended up in the back seat between Emma and Andrea. Stephanie sat on the front bench

beside Mia. The stable worker handed Mia
the reins.

"Thanks," Mia told him. Then she expertly
flicked the reins. "Walk on, Niki."

Soon the runners were sliding smoothly over
the snow. Mia guided the sleigh out of stable
yard and across the flat, open snowy ground of

Clover Meadows. Bells jingled softly on Niki's harness, and his hooves moved rhythmically through the snow. The cold winter wind whipped around the girls, but the blanket kept them toasty warm.

"This is fun!" Emma exclaimed. Her cheeks were pink, and her bright green eyes sparkled.

Olivia nodded. "Maybe afterwards we can go back to my house," she suggested.

"I can make us some cocoa and we can play the game some more."

Andrea and Emma traded a look. "Um, I probably have to go straight home after this," Andrea said.

"What? Why?" Olivia asked. In the front seat, Mia shrugged without turning around.

"I'm not sure I can make it either. I need to get home and walk my dogs."

Olivia was disappointed. "But I really need your opinions. I want to make sure my game works properly before I turn it in on Monday."

Stephanie turned around to face her.

"I'd come, but I'm much too *busy*." She pronounced the last word in the same exaggerated way as her avatar had in the game.

Olivia frowned. "Wait," she said, glancing around. Stephanie, Andrea and Emma were glaring at her. Even Mia was shooting disgruntled looks over her shoulder while she steered the horse. "Are you guys mad about those silly avatars?"

"Is that really how you see us?" Emma sounded hurt. "You made me look like an airhead who only cares about fashion."

Mia nodded. "And seriously, I try to brush off most of the pet hair before I go out."

"And I might like to keep busy, but I'm not as hyper as you made me look," Stephanie added.

Andrea rolled her eyes dramatically. "And I'm not a total diva," she sang out with a bunch of fancy trills at the end.

Olivia wasn't sure what to say. "It was supposed to be funny," she blurted out at last.

"I thought you guys would laugh."

Mia shrugged and fiddled with the reins. "I guess I didn't get the joke," she muttered.

Olivia glanced around. Now none of her friends would meet her eye. She felt her heart sink as she realized she'd made a big mistake. She'd wanted to laugh with her friends, but they thought she was laughing at them.

She shivered, suddenly feeling a distinct chill despite the warm blanket on her lap.

Late that night, Olivia's father opened her bedroom door. "Are you still up?" he asked in surprise.

Olivia looked up from her computer screen. "I'm fixing my game," she said. "I really want to get it finished tonight."

"Well, it's not a school night, so I suppose that's all right." Her father checked his watch. "But don't stay up too late, OK?"

Olivia nodded. But she knew she couldn't go to sleep until she'd finished the new programming. There was a lot more than a few extra-credit points at stake now.

The next day, Olivia paced back and forth on the carpet in front of the big window beside her front door. She paused every few steps to look outside, then checked her watch. Would they come?

She crossed her fingers, hoping her friends would show up. She'd sent an e-mail to all four of them first thing that morning inviting them

over to her house. The e-mail had explained that Olivia had made a few very important changes to Heartlake Adventure, and that she really wanted them to see what she'd done.

What if it didn't work, though? What if her friends didn't show up? Olivia wouldn't really blame them if they didn't. They'd seemed pretty angry the day before. It had made the rest of the sleigh ride very uncomfortable, which had only made Olivia feel worse. Even now that her game was finished, she was still ruining Stephanie's plans!

Scarlett ran into the room, her tail wagging. Olivia smiled at the dog.

"I ignored you all week, too, didn't I?" she said, bending to scratch Scarlett behind her floppy ears. "Sorry, girl. I'll take you out on an extra-fun walk to make up for it, OK?"

Scarlett's ears perked up at the word "walk."
She let out a sharp bark.

Olivia smiled. "Sorry, we can't go quite yet.
First I need to make things right with my
friends." She bit her lip. "I know you'll forgive
me no matter what, Scarlett. I'm not quite as
sure about them…"

Just then she heard the muffled chatter of
voices from the sidewalk in front of the house.
She rushed over to the window and looked
out. It was her friends!

Olivia smiled with relief as she watched
them round the corner of the picket fence,
which was almost buried in piles of snow.
But her smile quickly faded and her eyes
widened in amazement as she got a better look
at the four of them.

"What in the world…?" she murmured.

# 9
# Friends Again

Olivia threw open the front door as her friends hurried up the walk. Stephanie was in the lead. She was grinning.

"Here we are!" she called out, waving the clipboard she was holding. "Hurry up and let us in – I'm very busy, you know." She grabbed the whistle hanging on a string around her neck and blew a short, loud blast.

"Was that my cue?" Andrea pushed past her. She was dressed in a sparkly mini-skirt and carrying a microphone. "Everybody look at me!" she exclaimed in a dramatic voice. Then she started singing loudly, trilling up and down the scale.

Next Mia came forward. She had a puppy walking beside her on a leash and one of her pet bunnies cradled in her arms. Sitting atop her head was a fake bird.

"Let me through, you silly diva," she said, giving Andrea a playful shove. "I have animals to take care of!"

Finally Emma came into view. She was wearing a posh gown and a tiara with a sparkly jewel in the middle. At least a dozen necklaces were looped around her neck, and her snow boots had colourful ribbons tied on the laces.

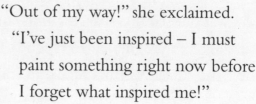

"Out of my way!" she exclaimed. "I've just been inspired – I must paint something right now before I forget what inspired me!"

Olivia's jaw dropped. At first she wasn't sure how to react.

Then Mia gave Andrea another shove and giggled. Andrea stopped singing and shoved Mia back, giggling even louder. Emma started twirling around pretending to paint in the air, which made Stephanie snort with amusement. Within seconds, all four of them were doubled over with laughter.

Cautiously, Olivia cracked a smile. Her friends did look pretty funny…

"Get it?" Stephanie asked, hurrying over and putting an arm around Olivia's shoulders. "This is our way of saying we're sorry."

"You're sorry?" Olivia swallowed back her laughter. "No, I'm the one who's sorry. I was trying to be funny, but I ended up hurting your feelings. I never wanted to do that."

Mia shook her head. "Those avatars were funny. We took things way too seriously yesterday."

"Yeah," Stephanie said. "We realized it as soon as we cooled off."

"Speaking of cooling off…" Andrea said, hugging her own bare arms.

"Oh! Come on in." Olivia led the way into the house. Then she turned to face her friends. "So you're not still angry?"

"We shouldn't have been angry in the first place," Emma said. "I guess we were just kind of sensitive. You know – because all week long, it seemed like you'd rather work on the game than spend time with us."

"That's what you guys thought?" Olivia was surprised.

Then she stopped to think about it. She really had been awfully caught up in the

game this past week. She'd forgotten about
the trail ride, then showed up late for Andrea's
concert…no wonder her friends had been
a little touchy!

"I'm really sorry," she said again. "Will you
guys forgive me?"

"Of course. As long as you forgive us, too."
Emma hugged her. Her tiara scratched Olivia's
ear a little, but Olivia didn't mind. "But you
really don't have to apologize. We know you'd
never make fun of us except in a friendly way."

Mia nodded. "We're sorry for overreacting."

"Thanks, you guys." Olivia's heart swelled.
She really did have the best friends in the
whole wide world!

"Friends again?" Stephanie asked with a smile.

"Always!" the other four said in unison.

"I still feel awful for making you guys feel
bad," Olivia added. "I think I figured out how
to show you that, though." She hesitated,
glancing around at each of her friends. "Will
you come in and try the new and improved
version of Heartlake City Adventure? I think
you'll like it much better than the old one."

# 10
## The Greatest Treasure

Soon the five friends were gathered once again around Olivia's father's computer. The familiar opening screen appeared.

"The graphics really look amazing, Olivia," Andrea said. "I noticed it on my avatar, too. You could see every feather on that boa!"

The others laughed. Olivia hit the Start button.

"Time to pick your avatars," she said.

Once again, there was an avatar for each of her friends. However, they looked very different than they had the day before.

Stephanie's clipboard and whistle were gone. Her movements weren't as fast anymore – now she moved at the same speed as everyone else. She was dressed in jeans and a sporty striped T-shirt, and her face held a big, friendly smile.

Andrea's avatar was wearing a cute aqua blue skirt and sparkly gold top. The microphone was gone and so was the diva attitude. She talked normally instead of singing every other word and she didn't dance or give dramatic monologues anymore, either.

Then there was Mia. All the pets were gone and her clothes showed no traces of animal hair. The only four-legged creature in sight was the horse drawing on the avatar's T-shirt.

Finally, there was Emma's avatar. She looked just as pretty and stylish as she did in real life. The ridiculous haute couture gown and

stiletto heels were gone, replaced by
a trendy purple mini-dress and sandals.

"Wow," Andrea said. "We look like…us."

"Yeah." Olivia smiled. "Go ahead and start
playing if you want."

Her friends' avatars weren't the only changes
Olivia had made to the game. As soon as the
others started moving their avatars through the
virtual city, another character appeared.

"Who's that?" Stephanie asked in surprise,
stopping her avatar.

Mia's eyes widened. "It looks sort of like…
Olivia!"

Olivia hid a smile. "That's me, all right."

The figure looked just like her, with the
same wavy chestnut hair and brown eyes. She
was dressed in a loose lab coat with pens,
a slide rule, and various other items sticking

out of the pockets. In her hands were
a microscope and a beaker of bubbling liquid.

"She looks like a mad scientist," Stephanie
said with a laugh.

"Look out!" the Olivia avatar exclaimed, stumbling forward. "I need to test my new invention!"

Avatar Olivia headed over to a virtual flower shop nearby. Several potted geraniums were decorating the sidewalk outside. Avatar Olivia dumped the beaker onto one of the plants, which immediately exploded. Olivia's lab coat and her whole face were black from smoke.

"Is she OK? Let's help her!" Andrea exclaimed.

"I've got an idea!" Emma quickly moved the mouse to send her avatar hurrying towards Olivia. She took out a powder compact from her stylish bag and removed all the dirt from Olivia's face with a powder puff.

"Whew!" Emma exclaimed. "It's much better now."

Olivia grinned. "Go ahead and keep playing…"

For the next few minutes, her friends moved their avatars all around the city, searching for the hidden objects Olivia had scattered throughout the virtual world. Every so often, Mad Scientist Olivia would turn up and need to be saved again. By the third time, when her beaker accidentally transformed a passing chihuahua into a monster the size of Godzilla, the five friends couldn't stop laughing.

"You're not like that, Olivia," Mia protested with a grin.

Olivia shrugged. "Maybe not quite that bad. But I did get awfully absent-minded about my friends this past week."

"Maybe a little," Stephanie admitted with a smile. "But it was worth it if it led to this. It's hilarious!"

"Yeah." Andrea sounded a little perturbed.

"But now our avatars seem totally boring."

Emma nodded. "Can't you change ours back to the way they were before?"

"Really?" Olivia was surprised. "You'd rather have the silly avatars back in the game?"

"Definitely," Stephanie declared. "Then it'll be perfect!"

And Stephanie was right. Olivia changed her friends' avatars back to the original versions – at least mostly. She adjusted things so that Stephanie's avatar didn't move quite so fast. And Emma's wasn't quite so dippy. And there wasn't quite so much pet hair flying off Mia's clothes. And Andrea didn't swan around quite so dramatically.

Ms Russell was so impressed that she let the entire science class play

Heartlake City Adventure for the last half hour of Monday's class. Everyone gathered around one of the classroom computers while people took turns trying out the game.

"This is awesome!" Jacob exclaimed as he manoeuvered the Stephanie avatar to pick up another puzzle piece. "But you should make me an avatar, too."

"Me too! Me too!" cried another boy. "Everyone says I'm way too clumsy. You could make me trip over my own shoelaces!"

"I have allergies," a girl called out. "You could make me sneeze all the time and blow the clues away before I can reach them." Jacob laughed. "That would be hilarious!"

Everyone started laughing and shouting out
ideas for their own avatars. The game was
a big hit with everyone!

Well, almost everyone. Chelsea was hanging back, looking peevish and unimpressed.

"I think it's ridiculous," she grumped. "Besides, who ever heard of making a computer game for extra credit?"

Ms Russell raised an eyebrow. "I think it's very creative," she said.

Just then Avatar Olivia turned a tree purple with one of her beakers, making everyone laugh. "Besides," added the teacher with a smile. "It takes a confident person to laugh at herself."

Olivia glanced at her friends, glad that they'd helped her figure out what a laugh it was to poke fun at herself. They all smiled back at her.

Just then Jacob picked up another clue from behind a column at virtual City Hall. "I think I've got all of them," he said excitedly. "Now what?"

Olivia stepped forward. This was her favourite part.

"You have to follow the map to figure out where to put the treasure together." She pointed to the corner of the screen.

Jacob clicked on the map icon. A little map of the city appeared in the corner.

He peered at it uncertainly. "I don't get it," he said. "It looks like it's leading me right into the harbour."

"Uh oh." Chelsea smirked. "Looks like Olivia made a big mistake in her game. Too bad."

129

Stephanie grabbed the computer mouse out of Jacob's hand. "Let me try," she said. "After all, it's my avatar."

"Bossy, bossy," Jacob said, rolling his eyes. "Just like your avatar!"

That made everyone laugh, including Stephanie.

"Go ahead, Stephanie," Ms Russell said. "Let's see if you can figure it out."

Stephanie nodded and moved the avatar forwards, following the map in the corner. The puzzle pieces Jacob and the others had found during the rest of the game drifted along with her.

"It really does look like it's leading into the harbour," Emma whispered into Olivia's ear. "It's not really a mistake, is it?"

Olivia smiled. "Just watch," she whispered back.

The avatar marched out onto one of the

docks in the virtual harbour. Stephanie
hesitated as she reached the water's edge.
She glanced at the map and shrugged.

"OK, here goes nothing," she said.

She moved the mouse, and the avatar
stepped off the end of the dock. For a second
it looked as if she was going to fall into
the harbour.

But suddenly, the puzzle pieces moved past
her, fitting together to form a large yacht!

"A boat!" Jacob exclaimed. "That's awesome!"

"Look," someone else called out. "The other
avatars are coming along for the ride!"

Sure enough, the other three avatars
appeared on the dock and climbed aboard.
Even Olivia's mad scientist rushed up,
accidentally blowing up the gangplank as soon
as she'd crossed. The yacht went chugging out

into the sunset with the picturesque view of Lighthouse Island in the background.

"Gorgeous," Ms Russell declared. "You did a fantastic job, Olivia. Not only was your game technologically impressive, but it was also a lot of fun."

"Thanks," Olivia said. "I had a lot of inspiration." She winked at her friends, who grinned back.

Meanwhile Chelsea frowned. "I thought the quest was supposed to lead to a treasure," she complained. "All we get is a silly boat ride?"

"Look at the name of the boat," Olivia said.

Stephanie leaned closer to see the name spelled out on the virtual hull. "Friendship," she read. "Is that the name of the boat?"

"Uh huh." Olivia shot all four of her friends a meaningful look. "And if you ask me, my friends are the greatest treasure I could have ever found."

## THE END

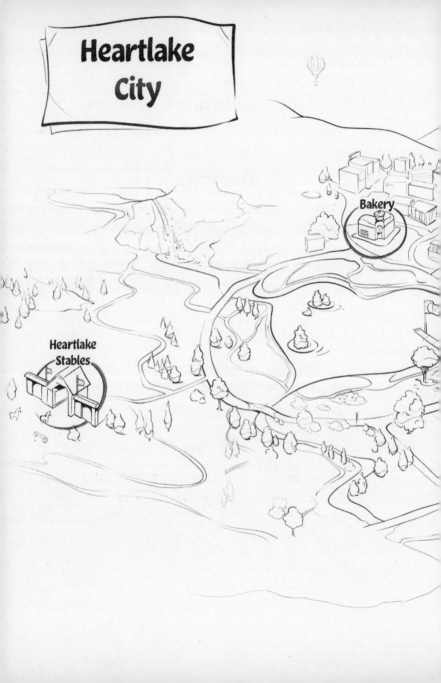

# Heartlake City

Bakery

Heartlake
Stables

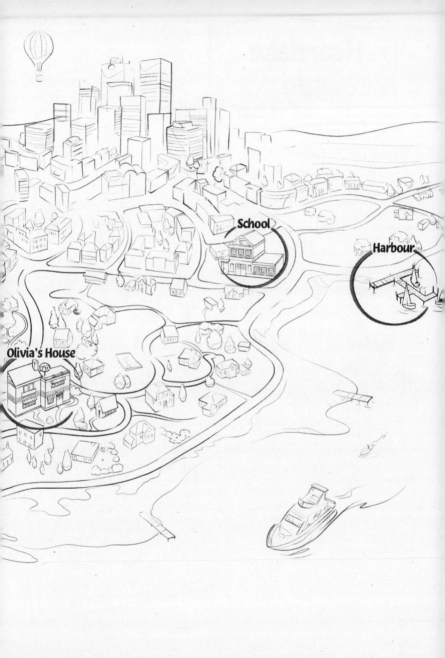

School

Harbour

Olivia's House

# Our Places

Take a closer look at the girls' favourite places in Heartlake City!

**Heartlake High**
All five girls attend the local school, Heartlake High. In the cafeteria the friends love chatting and planning their after-school meetings and activities.

**Café**
The café, with its cheerful red booths, is a cosy eatery where Andrea works part-time. It is the girls' favourite hangout – and Andrea's favourite place to perform karaoke!

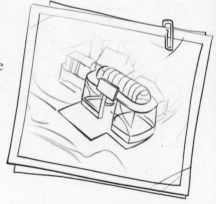

## Bakery

Cakes, cookies,
croissants . . . mmmm!
The Downtown Bakery always
smells of freshly baked yummy
treats. It's the best place to
warm up with hot chocolate and enjoy delicious muffins.

## Heartlake Stables

Everyone loves Heartlake
Stables. Mia takes part in
showjumping events. Emma
likes trekking on her horse.
Olivia is helping to tend
to a newborn foal. And
Stephanie loves organizing
winter sleigh rides.

## Harbour

Amber Sands beach has been
one of the girls' favourite
destinations ever since the
Dolphin Cruiser docked in
Heartlake Harbour.

# Pick Your Avatar

Olivia created some hilarious avatars for her game – but which do you think is the funniest?

**Andrea** - Dancing Diva

Dressed in a slinky rhinestone-studded mini-dress with a hot-pink feather boa around her neck, Andrea-Diva is a stage queen. Or rather a *drama* queen with her squeaky singing voice and madly twirling arms!

**Olivia** - Crazy Scientist

Beware of Olivia's bubbling liquid! This scatterbrained scientist is seriously accident-prone. She can't help investigating everything she sees, so don't be surprised if she turns her microscope on you!

## Stephanie - Team Leader

Speedy Steph is always in a hurry
so don't get in her way!
And make sure you do everything
to schedule, or you'll be at the
mercy of her whistle!

## Emma - Catwalk Star

Emma always wears the latest
styles from the world's best
fashion houses – including some
very wobbly stiletto heels! Watch
where you're going or she might
just paint a flower on you!

## Mia - Pet Lover

Mia is such an animal fan that she's
always surrounded by dogs, cats and
birds, and covered from head to toe
in pet hair and feathers – making her
look a bit like a scarecrow!

# Video Game Quiz

Follow the arrows to find out which type of video game suits you best!

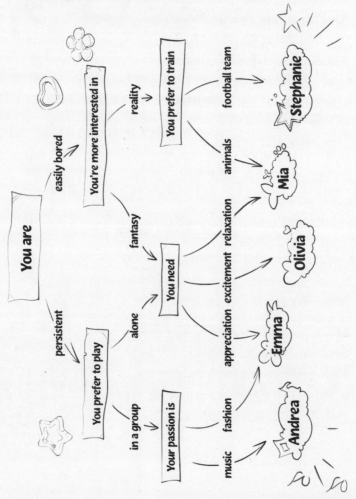

### Artificial Pets - Mia

A pet game that focuses on the care, raising, breeding or exhibition of virtual animals suits your interests and skills best. You'd make a good trainer of digital pets!

### Simulation - Stephanie

Since you have great organizational skills, you'd be best at simulation games. Coordinating different actions, building the best football team or even the whole city!

### Music Game - Andrea

If you enjoy dancing and singing like Andrea, you will love music games. Karaoke or dancing challenges are a great way to spend time with your friends!

### Adventure Game - Olivia

You have a scientific mind so adventure games would be the perfect choice. Decoding messages or exploring new locations will be a piece of cake for you!

### Makeover Game - Emma

If you like fashion like Emma you might try stylist games. Choose clothes, accessories and hairstyles and create some awesome projects.

# Winter Activities in the City

When it's cold outside there's nothing better than snowy activities with friends. Try out some of our tips below!

**Beautiful Decorations** – winter time is a perfect occasion to create sparkling cards, gift tags, room decorations or calendars. Use brocade, artificial snow, silver threads and paper to bring some winter magic inside.

**A Thousand Lights** – long, winter evenings will be magical if you decorate your room with strings of colourful lights.

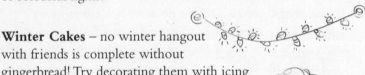

**Winter Cakes** – no winter hangout with friends is complete without gingerbread! Try decorating them with icing and colourful sprinkles.

**Cool Stories** – Try writing some cool stories to share with your friends over a cup of hot chocolate!

**Winter Pictures** – cheap, easy and inspiring! Blow on a cold window pane and doodle dream landscapes with your fingers!

# Memory Game

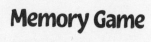

What do you remember about Heartlake City
from the story?

1. Where do the girls go for a hot chocolate on a chilly day?
   a) café
   b) bakery

2. Which horse from the Heartlake Stables takes the girls for
   a sleigh ride?
   a) Bella
   b) Niki

3. What is the shape of the HLC lake?
   a) clover
   b) heart

4. Where does Olivia's mum work?
   a) HLC hospital
   b) Heartlake High school

5. Andrea gives her winter concert in the:
   a) café
   b) Heartlake Theatre

Answers:

1. b   2. b   3. b   4. a   5. a